PEANUTS WISDOM TO CARRY YOU THROUGH

Published by Running Press,
A Member of the Perseus Books Group

Printed in China

Books published by Running Press are available at special discounts for bulk purchases in the United States by corporations, institutions, and other organizations. For more information, please contact the Special Markets Department at the Perseus Books Group, 2300 Chestnut Street, Suite 200, Philadelphia, PA 19103, or call (800) 810-4145, ext. 5000, or e-mail special.markets@perseusbooks.com.

ISBN 978-0-7624-5337-5
Library of Congress Control Number: 2013954530

9 8 7 6 5 4 3 2 1
Digit on the right indicates the number of this printing

Artwork created by Charles M. Schulz
For Charles M. Schulz Creative Associates: pencils by Vicki Scott,
inks by Paige Braddock, colors by Donna Almendrala
Designed by T.L. Bonaddio
Edited by Marlo Scrimizzi
Typography: Archer, Clarendon, Funkydori, Museo Slab, Quicksand, Univers

Running Press Book Publishers
2300 Chestnut Street
Philadelphia, PA 19103-4371

Visit us on the web!
www.runningpress.com
www.snoopy.com

PEANUTS WISDOM TO CARRY YOU THROUGH

Based on the comic strip, PEANUTS,
by Charles M. Schulz

RUNNING PRESS
PHILADELPHIA · LONDON

"Be yourself. No one can say you're doing it wrong."

—Charles M. Schulz

Be
BOLD

"You know, you don't have to fly south for the winter. Just because everyone else is doing it, doesn't mean you have to."

—*Snoopy*

Be
Vocal

"Throw it by 'im, pitcher! He can't hit it!"

—*Lucy*

Be
DISTINCT

Charlie Brown: I want to be liked for myself. I don't want to be liked because I know the right people. I want to be liked for ME!

Lucy: Who?

Be
Feisty

"Inscrutable? No, Ma'am . . . I can't spell inscrutable. You said if I took part in the spelling bee, all I'd have to do is spell words. You didn't say I'd have to spell 'em right!"

—*Franklin*

Be
EYE-CATCHING

"Every time they all go into the mall, I get left alone in the car. Sometimes people pass by and talk to me. Other times they just look at me like I'm different."

—*Snoopy*

Be DIGNIFIED

Be
Offbeat

Be
REAL

"The world is filled with beautiful plants and flowers, but I'm just an ugly weed. I'm a poor ugly weed trying to push her way up through the sidewalk of life!"

—*Peppermint Patty*

Be
OPINIONATED

Charlie Brown: It's really a good thing that people are different. Wouldn't it be terrible if everybody agreed on everything?

Lucy: Why? If everybody agreed with me, they'd all be right!

Be
Original

"I thought I was the life of the party when I put the lampshade on my head. But then everybody had to get into the act."

—*Snoopy*

Be
ODD

"Things change. In the old days you never would have seen a pirate waiting for the school bus."

—*Linus*

Be
ONE IN A
MILLION

"Snowflakes fascinate me. Millions of them falling gently to the ground. . . . And they say that no two of them are alike! Each one completely different from all the others. . . . The last of the rugged individualists!"

—*Snoopy*

Be
Clever

Be
SOMEONE

Charlie Brown: You're right, Lucy! You're right! You've made me see things differently. I realize now that I am part of this world. . . . I am not alone. I have friends!

Lucy: Name one!

Be
ARTISTIC

"What do you think?"

—*Lucy*

Be
PROUD

"Don't bother making any extra prints for me."

—*Snoopy*

Be
Noticed

Be
ATYPICAL

"I know what you mean. I'm not a joiner, either."

—*Snoopy*

Be
UNCOMMON

Peppermint Patty: My dad says that I am "a rare gem."

Charlie Brown: I agree with him.

Be
STRATEGIC

Peppermint Patty: Quick, Marcie, I need some answers! If you get your paper in first, you get extra credit. . . .

Marcie: Extra credit on a D-minus?

Be
Special

Lucy: There goes my brother with his stupid blanket.

Charlie Brown: Why do you let it bother you? Lots of kids have blankets that they drag around.

Lucy: How many have blankets that follow them!

Be
UNUSUAL

"If anyone saw me sitting here in the desert talking to a cactus, they'd say I was cracking up. What's wrong with talking to a cactus? Actually, he's pretty sharp."

—*Spike*

Be
BEAUTIFUL

Marcie: You don't want to look too beautiful.

Peppermint Patty: Sarcasm does not become you, Marcie!

Be
Charming

"For show-and-tell today I have something unique. I'm not going to tell about a pet or show you a toy or a book or something like that. Instead, I'm going to tell you all about someone I consider quite fascinating. Myself!"

—*Sally*

Be
ACCEPTING

"I have a strange team. . . ."

—*Charlie Brown*

Be Creative

Be
GIFTED

Be
COOL

Be
A BELIEVER

"Dear Great Pumpkin,
Something has occurred to me. You must get discouraged because more people believe in Santa Claus than you. Well, let's face it, Santa Claus has had more publicity. But being number two, perhaps you try harder."

—*Linus*

Be
Talented

Be
CONFIDENT

"Dogs are the best thing ever invented! We're the highest form of life on the earth! The world revolves around us!"

—*Snoopy*

Be
FUN

Be
Silly

Be
UNEQUALED

"Some of the guys over at the playground were discussing crabby sisters. Guess what . . . I won! They all agreed that I have the crabbiest sister in the neighborhood."

—*Rerun*

Be
Different

Charlie Brown: You want a dog? Here is just the dog for you!

Peppermint Patty: Where?

Be
TRENDSETTING

"Beagles should never wear down-filled jackets!"

—*Linus*

Be

YOU!